The Loud Bang

Written by Paul Collins

Illustrated by Trish Hill

sundance™

a black dog book

Published by
Sundance Publishing
One Beeman Road
Northborough, MA 01532

Copyright © text Paul Collins
Copyright © illustrations Trish Hill

First published 2001 by
Pearson Education Australia Pty. Limited
95 Coventry Street
South Melbourne 3205 Australia
Exclusive United States Distribution: Sundance Publishing

Guided Reading Level I
Guided reading levels assigned by Sundance Publishing using the text characteristics
described by Fountas & Pinnell in the book *Guided Reading,* published by Heinemann.

ISBN 978-0-7608-4995-8

Printed in China
06/09-225339

Contents

Characters

Shane likes to think
he knows everything
about everybody.

Jeremy is observant.
He loves mysteries.

Tina likes things
to be neat and tidy.

Kelly is Shane's sister.
She is full of energy,
and she loves being active.

Chapter One

Whoops!

We were on school vacation when it happened.
The mystery, that is.

Tina, Jeremy, Kelly, and I were worn out.

We had been playing tag all morning.

We ran and ran and ran.

Kelly was running so fast, she didn't see

the bucket of water until it was too late.

SPLASH!

Dad heard the splash.

He just finished washing his brand new car.

It was hot and he was getting cranky.

He came running toward us.

"You kids!" he said. "Inside now!"

"Whoops," I said.

Tina, Jeremy, Kelly, and I went inside.

There was nothing to do
so I got us some cool drinks.

We were sipping orange juice
when we heard a loud bang.

Chapter Two

Snoops

I jumped up to take a look out the window.
There was no one at the door.

"There's Mrs. Hepburn," I said.
She was walking by with her shopping cart.

Then I noticed the big yellow delivery van.

It was parked on the other side of the street.

Tina joined me by the window.

"It must have been the delivery van," I said.

The doorbell rang and Mom called out,
"I'm coming, I'm coming!"

"Delivery," I told Jeremy and Kelly.
"Mom gets loads of them. She works at home."

The window was open.

We could hear people cheering.

Kelly slurped her drink.

"I can hear people having fun out there,"

she said. "I wonder what they're doing."

"There's a group of kids playing baseball
in the park across the street," Tina said.
We looked out the window.

The park was small. A kid made a hit.
It bounced off the factory next door.

"Looks boring," I said. "In fact,
I'm bored already."

"Well, let's not sit in here all day," said Kelly.
"Let's go for a swim."

Chapter Three
The Discovery

Everyone got up.

"Dad might take us to the pool," I said.

"Maybe we can go in our new car."

We went out to the car to look for Dad.

We didn't find Dad,

but we did find something else.

Jeremy was the first to spot the crack.

It spread right across the headlight.

In the sunlight, it was like a silver spider web.

"Oh no," I cried. "Not Dad's new car!"

"Somehow, Dad's headlight got broken," I said.

"Well, we didn't do it," Jeremy said.

"We better tell your dad," he added.

"We don't want him to think we did it."

I shook my head.

"It's no use. He will think we did it," I said.

"No, he won't," said Kelly.

"Yes, he will," I said.

Tina rolled her eyes.

"We were playing around the car.

Your father knows that!" she said.

"And he did yell at us for
knocking over the bucket," I pointed out.
"He hates it when I play near cars."

"Well," said Kelly. "Let's look for clues!"

Chapter Four

The Detectives

We crowded around the cracked headlight.

The door was dented, too.

"Mrs. Hepburn walked past with a cart,"
I said.

We knelt down to get a closer look at the dent.

"The dent is up too high for Mrs. Hepburn's
cart," said Jeremy.

Suddenly, there was a loud thwack.

A baseball from the park flew over the fence.

It hit a tree in our front yard.

Kelly raced over and grabbed it.

"Let's see if it matches the dent!" she said.

But the baseball was too small.

"It still could have smashed the headlight,"
I said.

We looked closely at the dent.

"Look!" said Kelly.
"There's a smudge of paint here."

"It's yellow paint," said Jeremy.

I snapped my fingers.
"That delivery van was yellow!" I said.
"Let's tell Dad."

Chapter Five

Case Closed

"It wasn't the delivery driver," said Tina.

"He parked on the other side of the street."

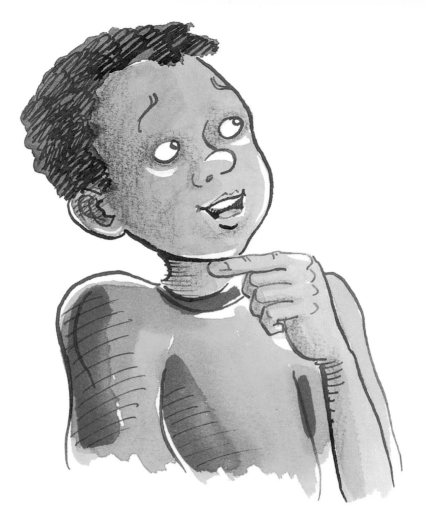

"Yes," I said.

"But we heard the bang before he parked.

We thought it was a knock at the door.

But that must have been when he hit the car."

"Of course," added Jeremy.
"Then he backed out and parked
on the other side of the street!"

"The mystery is solved!" I shouted.

Dad came over. He was looking pretty upset.

He was already staring at the dent!

"It wasn't us, Dad. But we know who did it!"

I said quickly.

"So do I," Dad said. He was having a bad day.
"The delivery driver just came to apologize,"
he added.

"I knew it all along," said Jeremy.

"Sure," said Tina.

"Hey," I said. "Now maybe Dad will take us to the pool!"